Dear Parents:

Congratulations! Your child is taking the first steps on an exciting journey. The destination? Independent reading!

STEP INTO READING® will help your child get there. The program offers five steps to reading success. Each step includes fun stories and colorful art or photographs. In addition to original fiction and books with favorite characters, there are Step into Reading Non-Fiction Readers, Phonics Readers and Boxed Sets, Sticker Readers, and Comic Readers—a complete literacy program with something to interest every child.

Learning to Read, Step by Step!

Ready to Read   Preschool–Kindergarten
• big type and easy words • rhyme and rhythm • picture clues
For children who know the alphabet and are eager to begin reading.

Reading with Help   Preschool–Grade 1
• basic vocabulary • short sentences • simple stories
For children who recognize familiar words and sound out new words with help.

Reading on Your Own   Grades 1–3
• engaging characters • easy-to-follow plots • popular topics
For children who are ready to read on their own.

Reading Paragraphs   Grades 2–3
• challenging vocabulary • short paragraphs • exciting stories
For newly independent readers who read simple sentences with confidence.

Ready for Chapters   Grades 2–4
• chapters • longer paragraphs • full-color art
For children who want to take the plunge into chapter books but still like colorful pictures.

STEP INTO READING® is designed to give every child a successful reading experience. The grade levels are only guides; children will progress through the steps at their own speed, developing confidence in their reading.

Remember, a lifetime love of reading starts with a single step!

Special thanks to Ryan Ferguson, Debra Mostow Zakarin, Kristine Lombardi, Rita Lichtwardt, Nicole Corse, Karen Painter, Stuart Smith, Sammie Suchland, Charnita Belcher, Julia Phelps, Julia Pistor, Renata Marchand, Michelle Cogan, Kris Fogel, Arc Productions, Andrew Tan, Alexandra Kavalova, and Genna du Plessis

Published in the United States by Random House Children's Books, a division of Penguin Random House LLC, 1745 Broadway, New York, NY 10019, and in Canada by Penguin Random House of Canada Limited, Toronto.

Step into Reading, Random House, and the Random House colophon are registered trademarks of Penguin Random House LLC.

Visit us on the Web!
StepIntoReading.com
randomhousekids.com

Educators and librarians, for a variety of teaching tools, visit us at RHTeachersLibrarians.com

ISBN 978-1-101-93986-4 (trade) — ISBN 978-1-101-93987-1 (lib. bdg.) — ISBN 978-1-101-93988-8 (ebook)

Printed in the United States of America
10 9 8 7 6 5 4 3 2

Barbie™
STAR LIGHT ADVENTURE

STAR SONG

Adapted by Apple Jordan

Based on the screenplay by
Kacey Arnold and Kate Boutilier

Illustrated by Charles Pickens
and Patrick Ian Moss

Random House New York

Barbie lives

on the planet Para-Den.

She takes care
of the animals
that live there.

Barbie has
a special skill.
She can move things
with her mind.

Barbie's father
gives her a message.
The king has
a job for her.

The stars are fading.
The king needs help.
He must reset the stars
to save the galaxy.

Barbie says goodbye
to her father.
She will go help
the king.

Barbie arrives on the king's planet.

She meets other people
with special skills.
They will work together
to save the galaxy.

The king has a machine
to reset the stars.

But first he must get
to the heart
of the galaxy.
The others will help.

Barbie and her friends
train for the mission.

The king gives
them a special test.
They must capture
a Starlian creature
and bring it to him.

Barbie and her friends
find the Starlian.

It is big.

It is scared.

Barbie drums on a tree.
The music calms
the creature.
It trusts Barbie.

The Starlian leads
the king's ship
through the galaxy.

The ship lands
on Central Planet.
The team works together
to pass through
a tricky field of orbs.

At last, they find the
heart of the galaxy.
The king sets up
his machine
to reset the stars.

But something is wrong.

The stars do not dance.

They begin to fall.

Barbie hears a song.

The friends sing along.

The stars begin
to flicker.

They begin to dance!

It is not the machine
that resets the stars.

It is Barbie
and her friends!
The stars are saved
by the song they
sing together.

BE TRUE
TO YOU

STARS
OF THE
GALAXY

REACH
STARS

Barbie